"There is simply no issue more important. Conservation is the preservation of human life on earth, and that, above all else, is worth fighting for."
—Rob Stewart

This book is dedicated to ROB STEWART, for showing me the way to help the sharks and the ocean.
—Zoë Williams

This is for ROBERT AROS, ESTELLE AROS, and ALYSSA AROS. I would like to thank my family for supporting and loving me throughout my life. I don't think any other family could've made me feel grateful, loved, and important, or make me laugh and smile as much as I do! I love each and every one of you very much!
—Sandra Aros

www.mascotbooks.com

Coral's Quest

For more information, please contact:
Mascot Books
620 Herndon Parkway, Suite 320
Herndon, VA 20170
info@mascotbooks.com

Library of Congress Control Number:
2019915186

CPSIA Code: PRT1119A
ISBN-13: 978-1-64543-326-2

Printed in the United States

FOREWORD FOR THE FUTURE

I am inspired by this story and Zoë's efforts for shark and marine conservation. I hope her work and this story gives readers of all ages a glimpse into the issues and see the problem from the animal's perspective. With an estimated 8 million metric tons of plastic entering the ocean every year, a significant amount of which is used only once before being thrown away, something needs to change.

If we continue down this path, we will have more plastic than fish in the ocean by 2048. Plastic does not go away—it only breaks into smaller pieces that can cause devastation when ingested by marine life. We are only beginning to understand how plastics can impact human health, as well. Every person can and does make an impact on the planet. If everyone took small steps to be mindful of what they choose to consume, that collective effort can make a difference for future generations of all species. Thank you, Zoë, and to those like her who share their time and talents to speak up for those without a voice.

Aloha,

Ocean Ramsey

Shark and marine conservationist and biologist
One Ocean Research, Conservation, & Diving

 @OCEANRAMSEY

Illustration inspired by photos taken by Juan Oliphant

@juansharks

Once there was a hammerhead shark named Coral. Her skin was a silky grey, she had beautiful fins, and her eyes were a sparkly blue. Coral lived in the Caribbean Sea. Coral was a happy shark, but one day she noticed her home wasn't as pretty as it used to be.

Her best friend was a parrotfish named Reef. She was sparkly yellow with sunset-colored fins and had turquoise markings that looked like they were painted on.

"REMEMBER WHEN YOU SAVED MY LIFE?" Reef asked Coral.

"I remember that!" Coral replied. "I discovered you tangled in a net. I bit as hard as I could to rescue you, and we've been best friends ever since," reminded Coral.

"I'm so glad you found me that day!" exclaimed Reef.

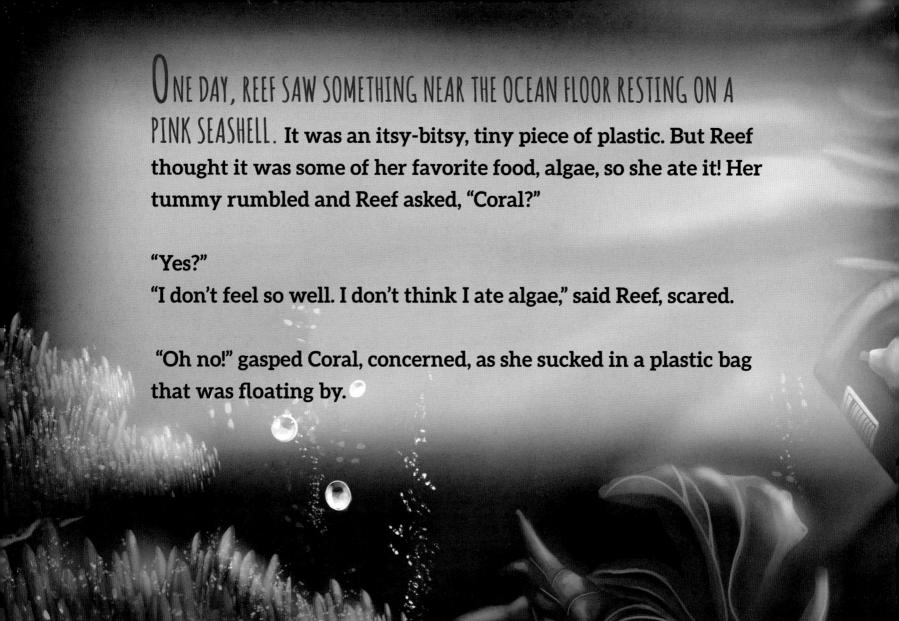

One day, Reef saw something near the ocean floor resting on a pink seashell. It was an itsy-bitsy, tiny piece of plastic. But Reef thought it was some of her favorite food, algae, so she ate it! Her tummy rumbled and Reef asked, "Coral?"

"Yes?"

"I don't feel so well. I don't think I ate algae," said Reef, scared.

"Oh no!" gasped Coral, concerned, as she sucked in a plastic bag that was floating by.

"Reef, I don't feel so good either. What's happening to us?" Coral asked.

"IT MUST BE WHAT THE HUMANS ARE PUTTING IN OUR HOME. It's making us sick," Reef said sadly.

Within seconds, Coral couldn't breathe and she felt like she needed to swim to the surface.

As she swam, she noticed that she was turning into a human!

Coral suddenly had long brown hair, seaweed for a dress, and a necklace made of coral. She didn't feel like herself in this new body. It was hard to swim and she wanted to turn back into a shark, but she couldn't.

CORAL SWAM TO THE SHORE AND WALKED INTO THE BIG CITY NEARBY.

This was very scary for her because it was really noisy. There were many people around her, and there were fast machines racing by her. She saw the streets were filled with trash. Coral thought and thought until she finally realized that it was the plastic and trash making Reef and herself sick.

CORAL DECIDED TO GO BACK TO THE BEACH. As she got closer, she saw a man who looked like he was covered in plastic. It seemed to drop from his body. There were many types of plastic: balloons, straws, bags, water bottles, forks, and spoons. He was strolling down the beach, leaving plastic on the ground behind him with every step.

As she passed him, she wondered why he was littering.

"Hi, my name is Coral. Why are you dropping plastic everywhere?" she asked.

The man looked back. "Hi," he replied. "My name is Utensil. I'm dropping plastic because I'm helping make the world easier for people. They use plastic for everything. THEY USE IT ONCE AND THEN THROW IT AWAY."

"Oh...okay," Coral said, concerned.

CORAL CONTINUED WALKING WITH UTENSIL, cleaning up the plastic he was leaving behind, when suddenly she discovered a baby turtle trapped in plastic soda rings. "Look, Utensil. See what all this plastic is doing?"

As Coral removed the plastic from the turtle, Utensil realized how bad all this plastic was.

"Maybe I should stop making plastic, but the people won't like it," he said.

SO, UTENSIL KEPT DROPPING PLASTIC AS HE WALKED AWAY. CORAL CONTINUED TO CLEAN UP THE BEACH.

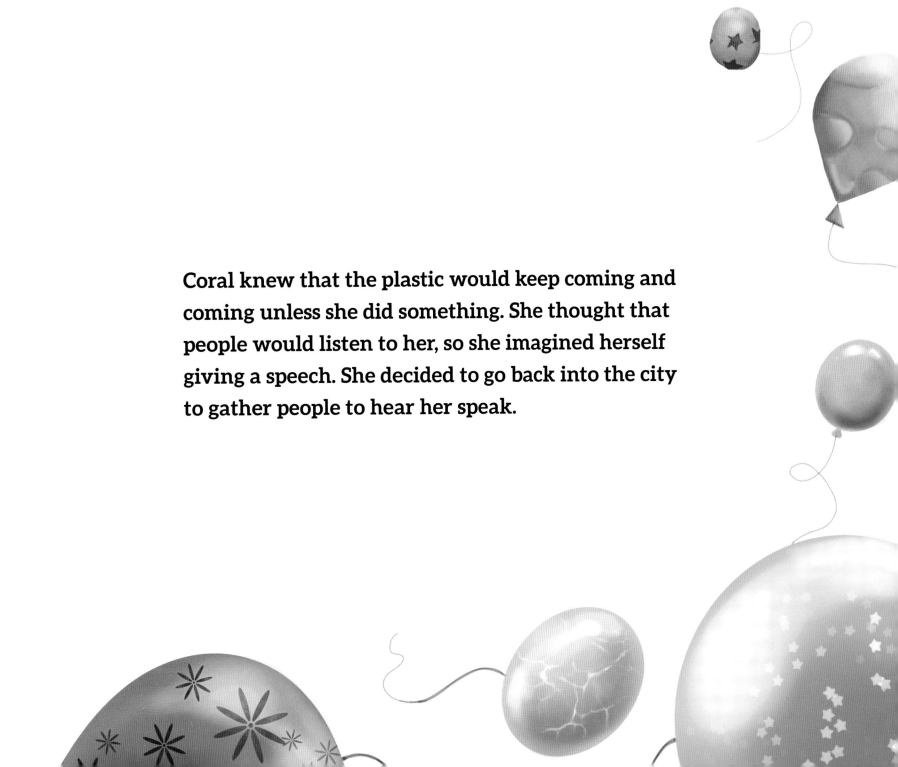

Coral knew that the plastic would keep coming and coming unless she did something. She thought that people would listen to her, so she imagined herself giving a speech. She decided to go back into the city to gather people to hear her speak.

Coral shouted with confidence, "the plastic is killing the earth and the animals.

It is so important that you stop making and using plastic. So, let's clean up this place! NO MORE PLASTIC!"

The audience clapped wildly.

Coral continued to give speeches all over the world. Soon people listened, and they stopped buying plastic. Even Utensil stopped making plastic, and, before Coral knew it, all the plastic was gone! CORAL WAS SO PROUD OF EVERYONE.

One day, while Utensil was closing his single-use plastic store, he saw Coral walk by.

"Hey Coral!" he shouted, as he raised his hand and waved at her. "I'm going to open a new store with all reusable items like metal straws, cloth shopping bags, metal water bottles, and bamboo forks, spoons, and knives. Thank you for helping me see that we can have a cleaner planet!"

Coral replied, "Sometimes it only takes one person to make a difference."

CORAL REALLY MISSED THE OCEAN, so she said goodbye to Utensil and went back to the seashore for a swim. All of a sudden, she turned back into a hammerhead shark!

As Coral swam deeper and deeper to the bottom of the sea, she noticed that her home was clean again. She found Reef swimming along the ocean floor.

"Reef! I'm so excited to see you!"
"Are you okay?" asked Reef anxiously. "I was so worried after you swam to the surface."

"I am so much better," replied Coral.
"What happened?"
"It's a long story, but I'll tell you later."
"Let's go for a swim!" exclaimed Reef, as she dashed away through the beautiful, blue water.

WITH CORAL'S HARD WORK, ALL THE OCEAN ANIMALS WERE HAPPY AND HEALTHY AGAIN, AND THE WORLD BECAME A MUCH MORE BEAUTIFUL PLACE WITHOUT PLASTIC.

ACKNOWLEDGMENTS

Thank you for supporting, donating, loving, encouraging, and believing in us and *Coral's Quest!*

A Wave of Thanks!

Juli Lasselle
Tadimdia Bridges
Mimi & Margaret
Heather Hughes
Emma Jones
Noelle Christensen
Eve Smyth
Kimberly StarKey
Mom & Dad, and Ash
Steve Oono
Sandra Coster
Mema & Papa
G-ma
Grandma
Grammy & Bapa
Ella Grace @EllaSavesTheOcean
Cash @TheConservationKid
Kalila Sayre Doctor
Miss Casey
Mrs. Dedrick
Mr. Ryan
Miss Kathleen
Mr. Tyler
Ms. Ferguson

Robert
Estelle
Alyssa
Kalie
Deeny
BJ, Eric & the kids
Bugs, Vero & the kids
Vu
Shawn & Jodi
Hannah & family
Kari
Ms. Louise
Grandpa & Liz
Jonathan Luke Stevens
Ocean Ramsey
Juan Oliphant
Captain Planet Foundation
Lonely Whale
One Ocean Diving & Research
Plastic Tides
Sharks4Kids
1 Piece Each
Team Sharkwater
Owl and Raven from Treehouse Books

Thank you for your generous donations!

M Global Services
Badger & Pen
Emma, Audrey & Claire
Ellie, Charlotte & Viv
Dr. Thaddeus Gala
The Lassesen Family
The Hughes Family
The Logan Family
Ada Christensen
Wilda & Walker Family
Athena Givens
Madison Sink
Ella Self
Yvonne Brautigam
Sharon C Anderson
Linda S Doran
Marc & Maureen Williams
Mike & Laura Naumes
The Phoenix Grange #779
The Hardy Family
Jane Anderson

And to all our family and friends for their love and support!

ABOUT THE AUTHOR

Zoë Williams is a ten-year-old native Oregonian who started her conservation awareness around age seven. She is committed to protecting sharks from shark finning and fishing, plus continuously reducing plastic pollution by doing local and beach clean-ups, and educating kids and adults through public speaking, art, music and writing. Zoë's dream is to continue her conservation work while going to school and preparing to become a Marine Biologist and Oceanographer. She would like to continue the Coral's Quest series in order to address more environmental issues.

@ SHARKSAREOURFRIEND

ABOUT THE ILLUSTRATOR

Sandra Aros grew up in California, but her love for art further developed when she moved to Oregon when she was eleven. She loves to illustrate children's books and paint art pieces. Ever since she was young, she was fascinated by the artwork in children's books and discovered in high school that she wanted to be an illustrator. What inspires her artwork is Disney films because she wants to capture the magical feeling people get when watching their films. Sandra Aros, a recent high school graduate, plans to pursue higher education in art in order to expand her illustration knowledge.

@ AROSPAINTBRUSH

Coral's Approved Beach Bag

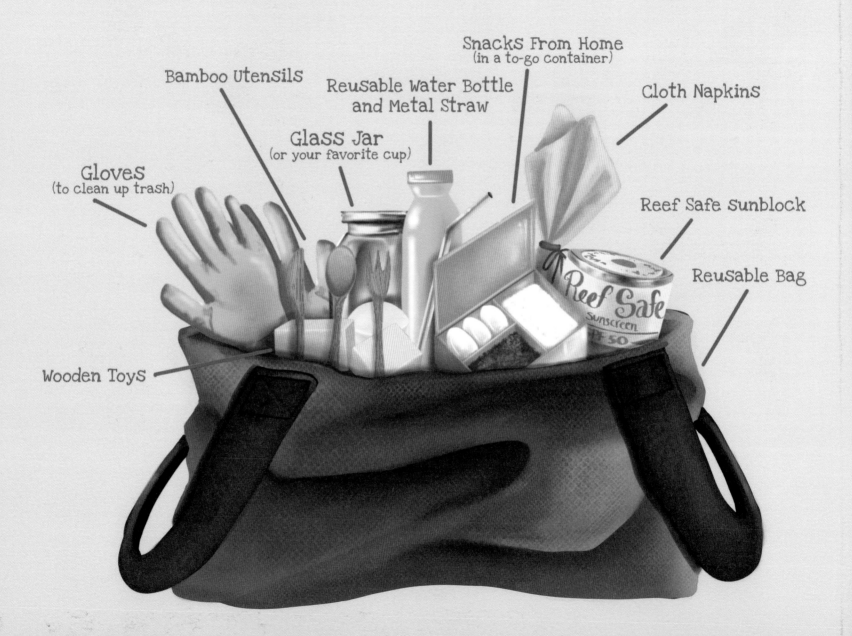

Gloves
(to clean up trash)

Bamboo Utensils

Glass Jar
(or your favorite cup)

Reusable Water Bottle
and Metal Straw

Snacks From Home
(in a to-go container)

Cloth Napkins

Reef Safe Sunblock

Reusable Bag

Wooden Toys

Reef Safe
sunscreen
SPF 50